The Cock
and
The Ghost Cat

The Cock
and
The Ghost Cat

Betty Jean Lifton

Illustrated by Fuku Akino

Atheneum   1965   New York

For Keiko and Eriko
who shall one day hear the little red cock

The Cock
and
The Ghost Cat

Once Upon A Time,

at the foot of a steep mountain in Japan, there lived an old farmer named Gembei, all alone with his red cock. Gembei loved the cock as if it were his own son. He brushed its bright red feathers until they glistened like a firebird's in the sun, and prepared the choicest morsels for it. Each dawn he waited in his bed until he heard the cock's beautiful "Ko-ke-ko-ko!" which is Japanese for "Cock-a-doodle-do!"

The villagers were also very fond of the little red cock, whom everyone knew as Koko. They could remember him when he was no more than a red ball of feathers, dancing up and down on legs that looked like tiny bamboo stilts, and so

young that his voice cracked when he tried to crow. But now there were none who would not willingly admit that Koko's deep-throated "Ko-ke-ko-ko!" was more exquisite than a thousand temple bells, and like Gembei, they did not rise in the morning until they heard it.

Now it so happened that in the wooded grove above Gembei's house there lived a wild ghost cat. Such cats are monstrous white creatures, as large as bulls, with the power to transform themselves into many forms. This one had noticed the delicious smells rising from Gembei's kitchen after the harvest; and one night, when a chill was in the air and the wind whistled mournfully among the trees, he crept down to look through the window.

The ghost cat's nostrils quivered when he saw the old man and the little red cock sitting by the fire with dishes of every variety spread in front of them—raw fish, seaweed, egg plant, cucumber, and bean paste cakes. Behind them, Gembei's shelves bulged with other delicacies. It was more than the ghost cat could bear to watch. He climbed back to his mountain den and, crouching there in the still night, he planned how to get rid of Gembei so that nothing would stand between him and the food on those shelves. At dawn he changed himself into a thin white kitten and made the slow descent down the mountain to Gembei's house.

Gembei was just preparing breakfast for himself and Koko when he heard a faint meowing outside his door. Opening it, he saw a pathetic little kitten, whose ribs stood out from hunger and neglect. "Saaah! What have we here!" exclaimed Gembei, his gentle heart filled with pity for the poor, helpless creature. He carried it quickly into the house and gave it a large pan of milk and rice. The kitten gulped everything down greedily and curled up in a warm corner of the kitchen to sleep. It was in this way that the wild ghost cat came to live in Gembei's house.

Of course it was only natural that the white kitten and the red cock should meet. The cat wet his lips at the sight of the plump, well-groomed bird, but Koko poked his sharp red

beak out so fiercely that the cat backed away. Besides, the cat knew how dear this handsome red cock was to the old man and realized that it would not be wise to make a meal of it just yet.

That night Gembei and the red cock and the white kitten had dinner together by the kitchen fire. Gembei generously piled his two little companions' plates even higher than his own. The kitten purred contentedly when he was finished. "What a nice new brother you have," Gembei told Koko. "Be sure that he is comfortable while I am gone." Then he took down his towel and soap and went out to the public bathhouse for his regular hot bath and chat with his friends.

"I have two sons now instead of one," he announced gayly to the other men as they sat chin deep in the steaming water. "I will have to work twice as hard to keep my little family going."

However, while Gembei was away, the white kitten and the red cock eyed each other suspiciously. Then the kitten crept into a dark corner of the bedroom and began sharpening his claws against a wooden chest. The sound—ga ree, ga ree, ga ree—was very much like that of a tiger preparing himself for battle in the jungle. Koko, who was in the courtyard waiting for Gembei, heard it and understood that this cat could not be trusted. After Gembei returned from the bathhouse, Koko hid himself inside the bedroom and waited in the darkness to see what the cat would do.

It was just about midnight, when Gembei was sleeping soundly, that the kitten changed himself back into his monstrous shape as a ghost cat. His eyes gleamed like two flaming coals, and his pointed teeth flashed like a row of naked swords as he moved closer and closer to Gembei. But just as he was about to spring, the red cock jumped forward bravely, crow-

ing: "Ko-ke-ko-ko! Ko-ke-ko-ko! The cat is going to kill Gembei!"

Gembei leapt up at the sound of his cock's familiar "Ko-ke-ko-ko!", thinking it was dawn, but the white ghost cat immediately changed itself back into a tiny white kitten and fell down on his cushion as if asleep.

All the oil lamps in the village went on, even some of the cooking fires, and you can imagine everyone's surprise when

they opened their shutters and saw that it was still the middle of the night, not dawn at all. The villagers climbed crossly back into their beds. The next morning they came to Gembei's house and shook their heads at the irresponsible bird who had so thoughtlessly awakened them. Nevertheless, Koko walked among them proudly, his red comb held high like a crown on his head, as though nothing were wrong.

"Perhaps my dear little red cock had a dream that it was dawn," Gembei said, apologizing for Koko. "Such things can sometimes make one cry out in the night."

That evening when the old man was again chatting with his friends in the bathhouse, the kitten again began sharpening his claws—ga ree, ga ree, ga ree—and Koko again hid himself inside the bedroom. At midnight, while Gembei was sleeping, the white kitten turned himself back into a frightful ghost cat. But just as he was about to spring, Koko once more jumped up crowing frantically: "Ko-ke-ko-ko! Ko-ke-ko-ko! The cat is going to kill Gembei!"

Once more all the villagers got up thinking it was dawn, and the white kitten fell down as if asleep. Gembei, himself, was quite puzzled and sat looking at Koko for a long time. "Why do you awaken so early, my little one?" he asked him. "See, your brother is still sleeping quietly. So should you be until the dawn."

The little red cock hung his head. He was very sad because no one could understand him, especially his beloved Gembei whom he was trying to save.

Gembei had to listen to many complaints against Koko during his next trip to the bathhouse.

"I was so tired today I could hardly work my fields," grumbled a farmer.

"I did not have enough strength to climb the mountain for firewood," mumbled a charcoal burner.

"I fell asleep at my wheel," groaned a potter.

Gembei tried to reassure them as best he could. "Perhaps my little red cock ate something that disagreed with him," he replied. "Such things can make one cry out in the night. But I am certain he will not crow again before dawn."

However, that same midnight the little red cock did crow again; and the midnight after. Each time as Koko cried out and Gembei woke up, the cat turned back into a kitten and fell down feigning sleep. And each time as the lights went on in the village, the villagers muttered angrily because their valuable rest was being disturbed.

It was early on the fifth morning of these unusual events that a group of villagers held a secret meeting at the shrine, and then two of them marched straight to Gembei's house. They did not smile in greeting as they entered, and they sat nervously by the charcoal brazier, ignoring the tea that Gembei carefully served them.

"It is our unpleasant duty to tell you . . . ," began the first, but his voice failed him before he could finish.

"We are sad to inform you . . . ," began the second, but he too could not go any further.

"Do not be afraid to speak up," Gembei encouraged

them kindly. "I am listening."

"Well then," said the first with more courage, "we are here to tell you on behalf of the village that you must get rid of the little red cock."

"Yes," said the second, "it has been decided that you must take him to the river to drown."

"Drown!" gasped Gembei, unable to believe what he had heard.

"Drown!" repeated the two men. And then they gulped down their tea noisily, as if to drown out their own words.

Gembei pleaded with the villagers to give Koko another chance. "Surely he has served us all faithfully these many years," he said. "And I promise you that if he crows at midnight one more time, I shall take him to the river without your asking."

The villagers agreed reluctantly, on hearing Gembei's pledge.

That evening Gembei did not go to the bathhouse, but stayed at home to speak to his little red cock. They sat together by the fire, as they had so often in the past, but this time Gembei spoke with special urgency in his voice.

"I am an old man and I have had no one but you, my dear little Koko," he said. "Never have I asked anything of you before, but I ask this now—please do not crow again in the middle of the night. If you do, I am powerless to save you."

The little red cock did not look up, but merely stared into the fire, as if his heart, like the logs, was turning into ash with every word Gembei uttered.

Deep in the shadows the white kitten purred with satisfaction. He knew that this night he would achieve his purpose, for the red cock could not be so foolish as to throw away his own life for the old man's. The cat watched as Gembei rolled his bed down on the floor and waited impatiently for his heavy breathing. Then he began sharpening his claws—ga ree, ga ree, ga ree—and just at the stroke of midnight, he changed into his real form and made ready to spring.

However, the little red cock did not hesitate a moment. Like a loyal retainer leaping into battle for his master, he cried out: "Ko-ke-ko-ko! Ko-ke-ko-ko! The cat is going to kill Gembei!"

The cat, poised in mid-air above Gembei, changed back into an innocent white kitten, and fell down as if asleep.

Immediately all the lights in the village went on. Then they went off again. Only Gembei's stayed lit. He knew what he had to do. Silently he packed some rice balls in a small wooden box and took a straw mat from the closet. Then stooping down, he tucked Koko under his arm and started off for the river with him. The white kitten sat in the window watching, a smug leer twisting at his lips.

When they arrived at the river bank, it was still dark. The sky was overcast with clouds, as if the moon itself did not want to witness what was happening. Gembei placed the straw mat on the water and set his precious cock on top of it. He put the box of rice balls at Koko's side.

"Farewell my dearest friend," he whispered, his sorrow too deep for tears. "I never thought we would part in this way. I promised to take you to the river, but I hope that somehow this straw mat and food will save your life. If not, perhaps someday we shall be reunited on another shore more kind than this one."

And unable to say more, Gembei stumbled off toward his house without looking back.

The little red cock was numb with grief as he watched his dear master go. He did not care about his own life, only Gembei's. If only he had been able to make him understand those words: "Ko-ke-ko-ko! Ko-ke-ko-ko! The cat is going to kill Gembei!"

As Koko floated down the river on his straw mat, it came to him that his only chance of saving Gembei now was to cry out his warning in the hope that someone who could understand would hear. And so as the icy waters swirled around him in the blackness, he pulled himself up and crowed with all the strength in his tiny body: "Ko-ke-ko-ko! Ko-ke-ko-ko! The cat is going to kill Gembei!"

All along the river bank the lights went on in the houses that he passed. Shutters opened, and then slammed closed impatiently when the people realized that it was not yet day. But still the little cock continued to call: "Ko-ke-ko-ko! Ko-ke-ko-ko! The cat is going to kill Gembei!" Over and over again he crowed, neither eating nor sleeping, until he was so weary he lay in a heap of wilted red feathers, like a flower with a broken stem.

"Just listen to that crazy bird crowing all the time!" people would exclaim as they saw him drifting by. "No wonder his master got rid of him."

However, a few hours after sunrise, when Koko was so feverish he could hardly lift his head to crow, a wandering monk passed by playing a flute. He was a holy man who had given up all possessions on this earth to devote himself to helping others. Over his thin body he wore only the roughest hemp robe, and over his shaven head he wore a straw basket so that his mind would not be distracted by earthly concerns. By now this monk had become so pure of heart that he could understand the language of animals. He let the flute

fall from his lips when he saw Koko floating by and heard the haunting cry: "Ko-ke-ko-ko! Ko-ke-ko-ko! The cat is going to kill Gembei!"

"Ho there!" he called, and reaching out he grabbed a corner of the mat and pulled its strange occupant to shore. "What is that you are saying, little red cock?"

Koko was so weak he could speak only with the greatest difficulty. "Hurry sir," he gasped. "The cat . . . is . . . going . . . to kill . . . my master . . . Gembei!" And after telling the holy man the name of his village, the little cock fell unconscious on the mat.

The monk placed the poor limp bird under his robe where it would be warm, and hurried to Gembei's village. Night had already fallen when he found the house. He hid the cock in a soft bale of straw in Gembei's courtyard, and knocked on the door.

An old man, his face lined with sorrow, looked out, and from behind him peered the sinister eyes of the ghost cat.

"Pardon me," said the monk, "but I have walked many miles and can go no farther. May I stay under your roof with you tonight?"

"You are welcome to my humble home," replied Gembei. "I only wish it were more grand for a holy person like yourself."

Gembei led the priest in by the warm fire and sat him in the little red cock's old spot. The white kitten watched intently from the other side of the room and for the first time did not come when Gembei beckoned for him. Although Gembei tried many ways to coax him over, he merely arched his back and kept his distance.

"Poor thing," said Gembei. "He must be lonesome for his brother, a little red cock who is no longer with us. I did not realize that he would miss him so much."

The monk said nothing, but drank the warm soup that Gembei made for him. He also ate his rice and boiled fish without a word.

"I wish I had a special room to offer you," apologized Gembei, laying his guest's bed down on the floor next to his own. "But at least my little red cock will not disturb you in the middle of the night. He will not bother anyone again." And Gembei's voice choked up even as he spoke.

"I sleep soundly," said the monk. "Nothing ever wakens me unless it be an earthquake."

The kitten crept into a far corner of the room as Gembei fell into an exhausted sleep. The monk kept his head down in the cotton quilt in such a way as to keep his eyes on the cat.

It was just a little before midnight when the white kitten rose stealthily, and satisfied that Gembei and the monk were deep in slumber, began sharpening his claws—ga ree, ga ree, ga ree. His ragged ears twitched with delight when he realized that neither man was stirring. Then taking advantage of Koko's absence, he changed into his huge monster shape and sprang upon Gembei.

But at that very moment the monk leapt up with the cry,

"Araaa! You scoundrel!", and grabbed him. Gembei opened his eyes in amazement to find his guest struggling on the floor with a huge white ghost cat.

The holy man, of course, was used to subduing wicked creatures. It wasn't long before he had the cat's legs bound together in such a way that it could not escape nor turn itself into anything else. The cat glared at the monk, but it lay quietly, knowing it was defeated.

Then the monk helped Gembei up from his bed and told him how he had found the little red cock floating on the water. "Your faithful bird was trying to warn you about this evil cat," he said. "But you took the wrong one down to the river."

Gembei followed the monk out into the courtyard where

the little cock lay, still unconscious, in the straw bale. Gembei could not bear to see his lovely bird in such a pitiful condition; but Koko, stirring at his touch, was so happy to see his master still alive, he managed to lift himself up and give a hoarse "Ko-ke-ko-ko!" Then he fell back into Gembei's arms and died peacefully.

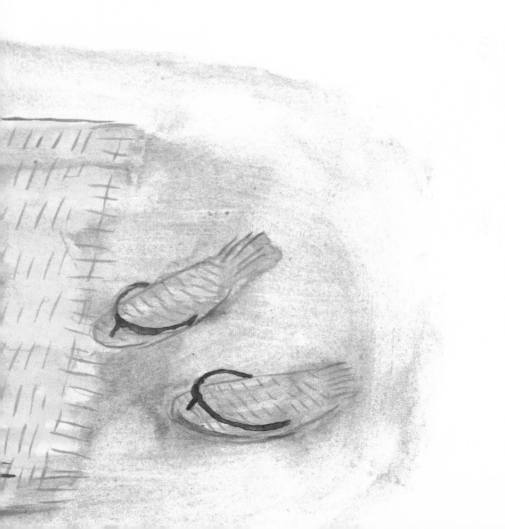

Immediately, on hearing "Ko-ke-ko-ko!", all the villagers turned on their lights, thinking it was dawn. When they saw that it was still dark, they marched furiously to Gembei's house. "What is the meaning of this?" they cried. "You promised to get rid of that cock!"

The villagers were stunned when they heard the true story about the little red cock. In fact, they became so enraged at the wild ghost cat's treachery, that they themselves dragged him down to the river.

The priest helped Gembei and the villagers erect a lovely statue of the little red cock right in the center of the village square. People came from miles around to view this brave bird who had so willingly given his life for his master. And even the Emperor sent a messenger with presents to Gembei when he heard of this noble deed.

But the little red cock seemed happiest when there were children playing at his feet and he could hear them calling merrily to each other: "Ko-ke-ko-ko! Ko-ke-ko-ko! The cat is going to kill Gembei!" Then his bronze feathers seemed to glisten in the sun just as in days of old, and it seemed that he might once again strut amongst them.

There were those who actually claimed to have seen the little red cock in Gembei's courtyard at different hours of the day and night; but everyone agreed that sometimes at dawn,

when the wind blew a certain way, they could still hear his deep-throated "Ko-ke-ko-ko!"—and that it was even more beautiful than it had been before.